Yoko Tanaka

DANDELION'S DREAM

Dedicated to Dan

❖

Special thanks to my London crit group: Bridget Marzo, Layn Marlow, Heather Kilgour, Cliff McNish, Andrew Weale, Jane Porter, Anne-Marie Perks, Loretta Schauer, Candy Gourlay, Joseph Coelho, Charles Wilkinson, and Patrick Miller; and to Emma Lawlor and Jo Haas.

First published 2020 by Walker Books Ltd
87 Vauxhall Walk, London SE11 5HJ

10 9 8 7 6 5 4 3 2 1

© 2020 Yoko Tanaka

The right of Yoko Tanaka to be identified as the author and illustrator of this work has been asserted by her in accordance with the Copyright, Designs and Patents Act 1988

Printed in China

British Library Cataloguing in Publication Data: a catalogue record for this book is available from the British Library

ISBN 978-1-4063-8877-0

www.walker.co.uk

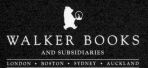

WALKER BOOKS
AND SUBSIDIARIES
LONDON · BOSTON · SYDNEY · AUCKLAND

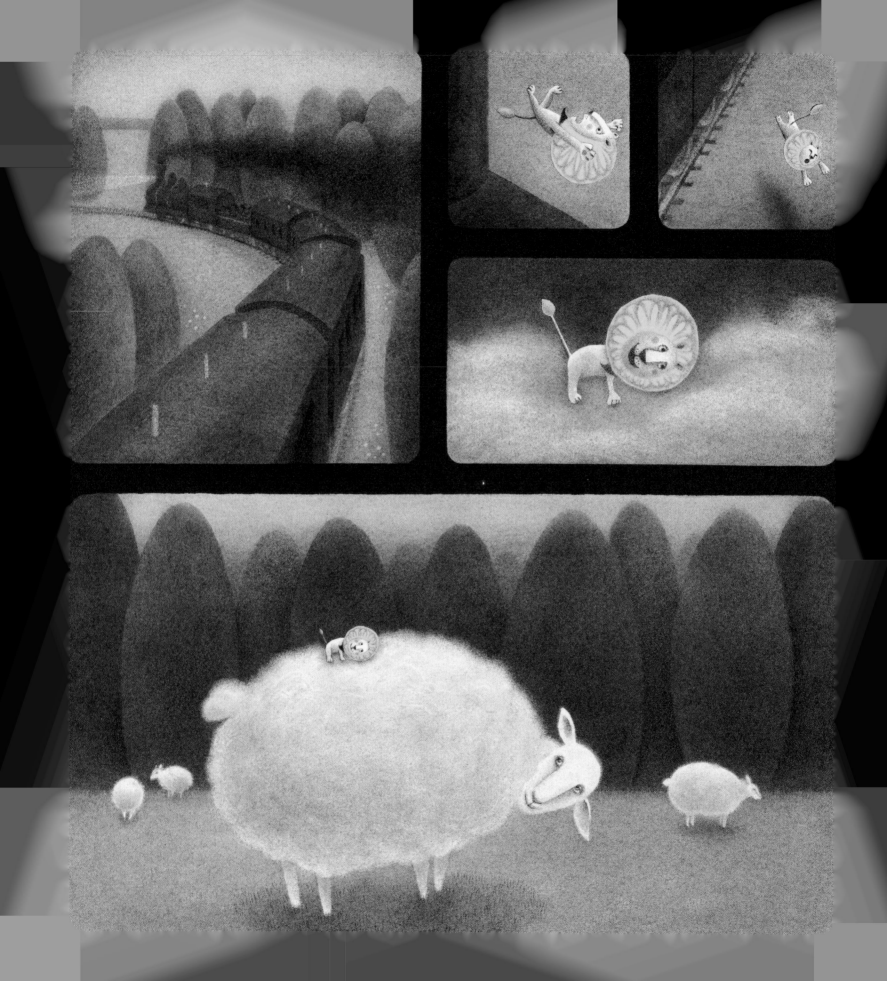

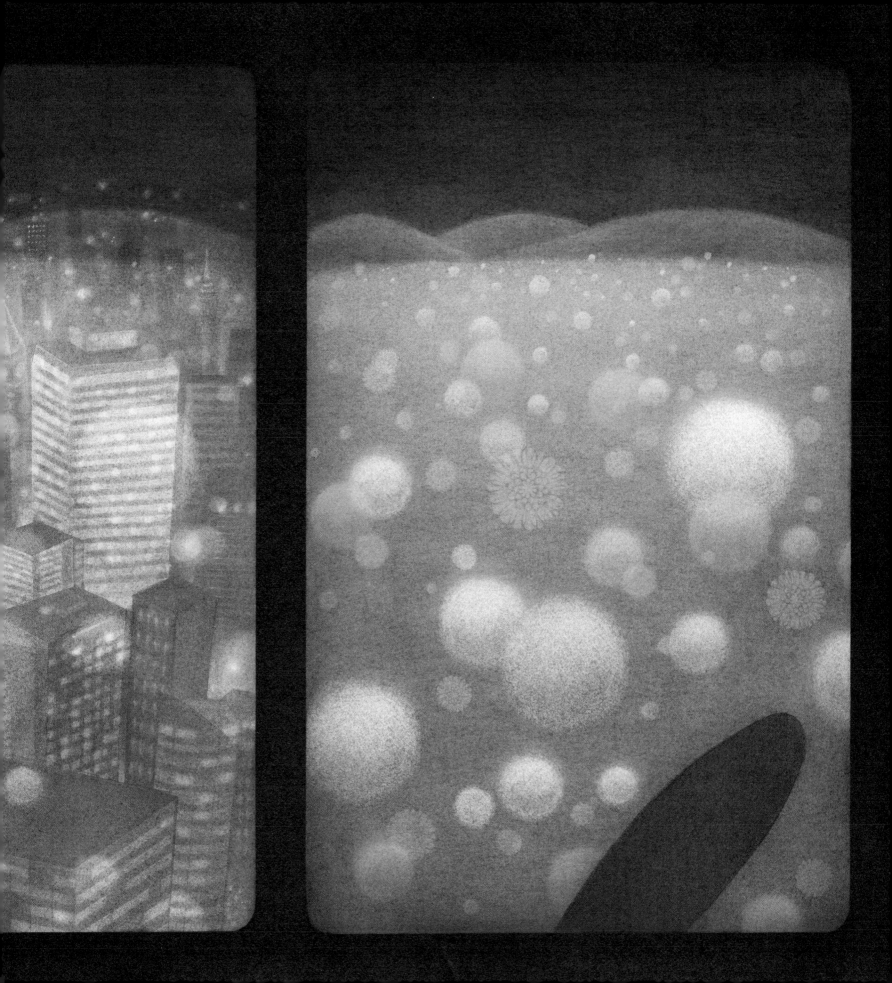

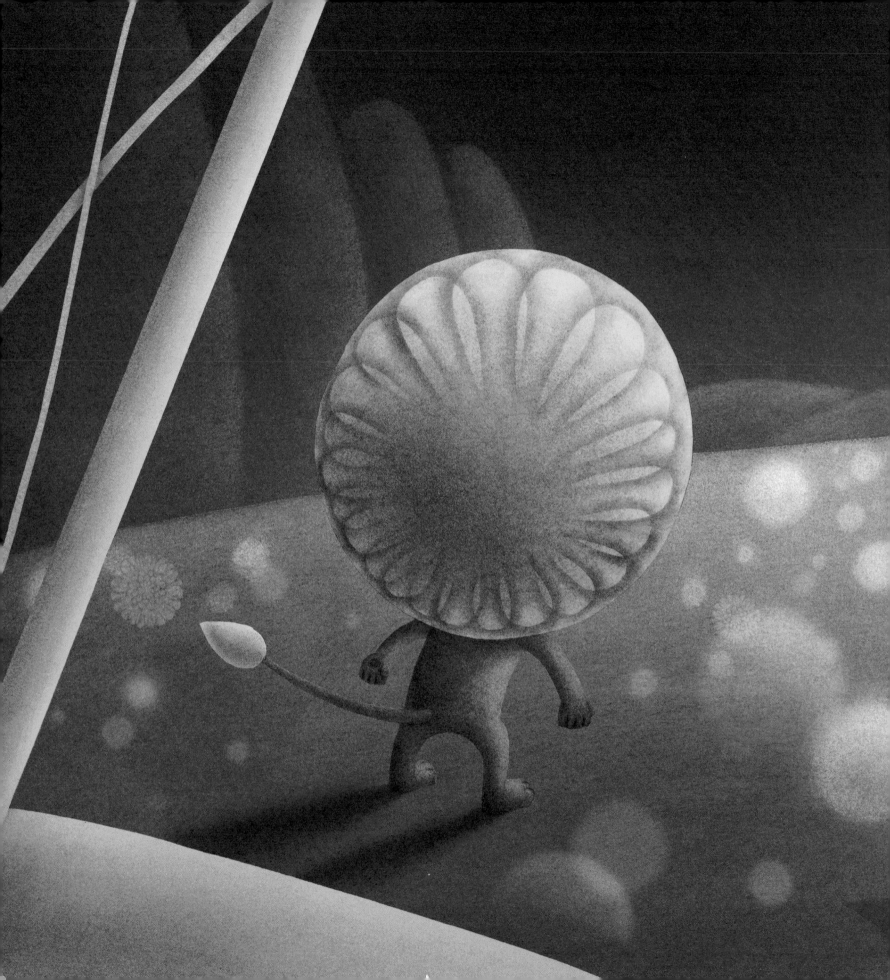

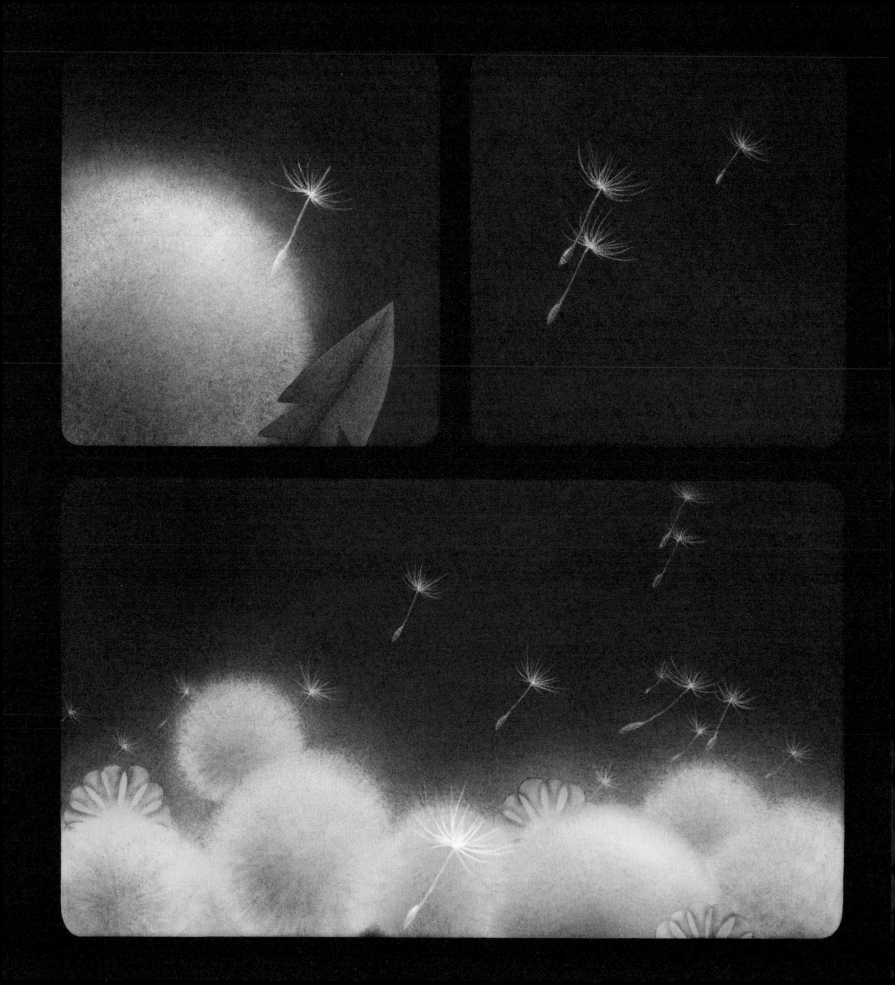

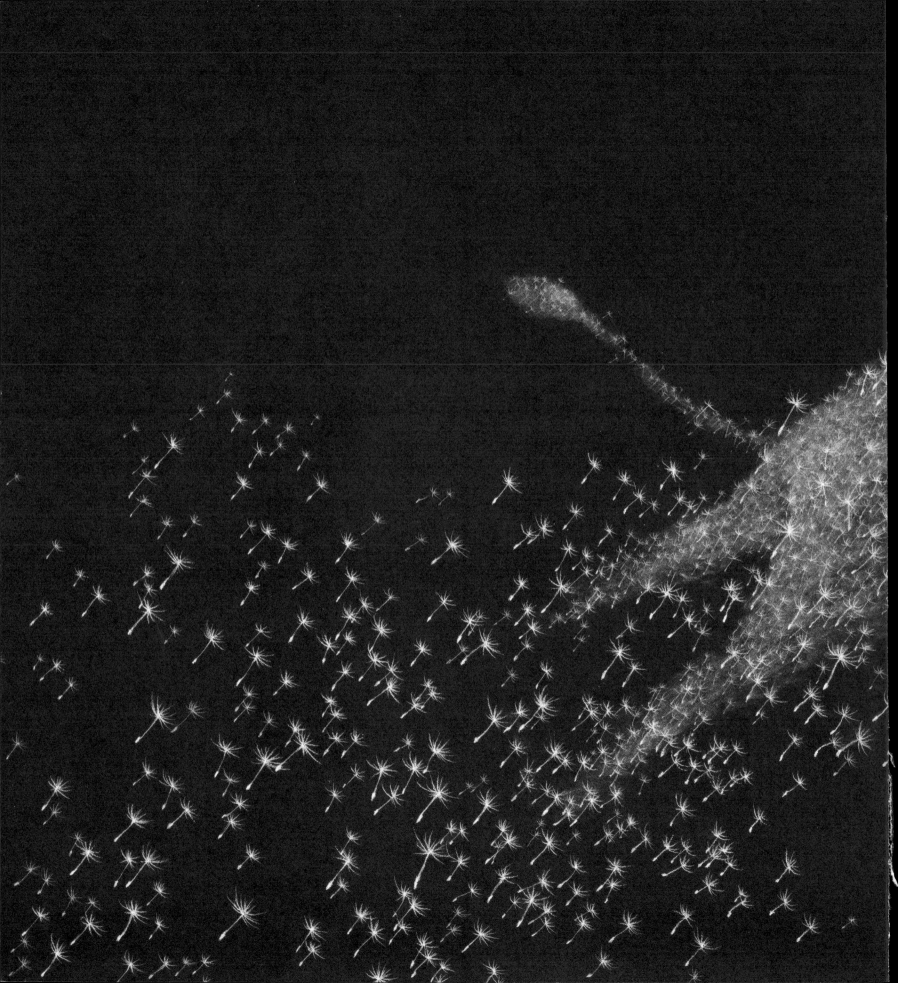